# RYAN VS ROBOT

## RONIN WING

ISBN: 978-1-7373604-2-1 (eBook)
ISBN: 978-1-7373604-3-8 (hardcover)

First Edition Book, September 2021

Book cover design, illustration, editing, and interior layout by:

www.1000storybooks.com

www.luminousfragmentspublishing.com

The robot army marched on, just ahead.

The lasers flew right over Ryan's head!

Ryan ducked—that sure was a close one!

The young boy hero fired his gun.

"No, no, no, Ryan! That is NOT fair!

I shot you first, from way back there."

"You are wrong, Robot. That is not how this goes.

The game is simple: you can't kill the heroes!"

Marcel just left, and Ryan frowned.

"Well, I don't need you around!"

As his frown faded, Ryan shook his head.

"I'm bored...I should've been nicer, instead."

Things would be different the very next day:

Beep, boop!

Ryan the robot was ready to play!

A new hero appeared to fight robots away.

A new story begins—it's Marcel's turn, today!

It didn't take long before more kids joined the game.

Soon, the robot wars would never be the same.

The war waged on! Lasers flashed across the sky.

And when that day ended, the kids said goodbye.

Marcel and Ryan were team leaders, you see.

And they became the best friends that friends could be.

"But," you say, "they can't still be friends.

That war was years ago."

Ah, but the game of friendship never ends.

Trust me—a robot would know.

CPSIA information can be obtained
at www.ICGtesting.com
Printed in the USA
LVHW070830301121
704816LV00002B/77

9 781737 36043